Just Us Three

First published in Great Britain by HarperCollins Publishers Ltd in 1996
10 9 8 7 6 5 4 3 2 1
First published in Picture Lions in 1996
10 9 8 7 6 5 4 3
Picture Lions is an imprint of the Children's Division, part of
HarperCollins Publishers Limited, 77-85 Fulham Palace Road, Hammersmith, London W6 8JB
Text copyright © Tony Bradman 1996
Illustrations copyright © André Amstutz 1996
A CIP catalogue record for this title is available from the British Library.
The author and illustrator assert the moral right to be identified as the author and illustrator of the work.
ISBN: 0 00 198049-1 (hardback)
ISBN: 0 00 664405-8 (Picture Lions)
Printed and bound in Hong Kong

Just Us Three

Tony Bradman
Illustrated by André Amstutz

PictureLions
An Imprint of HarperCollinsPublishers

We're three good friends – one, two, three,
I'm Alice, I'm Jack and he's Dan –

We meet every morning at a quarter to eight,
Our mums go to work and they mustn't be late!

We're three good friends – one, two, three,
I'm Alice, I'm Jack and he's Dan –

We all bundle in and we shout... HELLO!
To our favourite minder, Auntie Flo!

Time for a drink and a game or two...

Flo's terrific at...

We're three good friends – one, two, three,
I'm Alice, I'm Jack and he's Dan –

We're off to the park
where we can ride,

And SOAR on the swings...

and WHOOSH down the slide!

We're three good friends – one, two, three,
I'm Alice, I'm Jack and he's Dan –

Back past the shops, down a busy street,
To A GREAT BIG PUDDLE
where we STAMP our feet.

We're three good friends – one, two, three,
I'm Alice, I'm Jack and he's Dan –

Time for some lunch, with a GLUG and a SLURP,
And a WHOOPS and a SPLAT and a...

Now we're feeling tired and cranky too,

So it's BIFF, BASH and OWW!
and a loud...

But... we're three good friends – one, two, three,
I'm Alice, I'm Jack and he's Dan –

Flo reads a story and we snuggle on her lap,
And we SUCK and we NOD
and we have a nap.

We're three good friends – one, two, three,
I'm Alice, I'm Jack and he's Dan –

And when we wake up
we play hide and seek...
Who's under there?

Time for a snack
and our favourite game.

CHUFFA-CHUFFA, TOOT!
ALL ABOARD OUR TRAIN!

We're three good friends – one, two, three,
I'm Alice, I'm Jack and he's Dan –

The day's nearly over,
TICK-TOCK goes the clock,
Who's at the door with a
KNOCK, KNOCK, KNOCK?

Our mums have arrived so it's time to go...

BUT WE'LL BE BACK TOMORROW, AUNTIE FLO!

We're three good friends – yes, just us three!
I'm Alice, I'm Jack and he's Dan –

Here are some more Picture Lions

Quentin Blake's
ABC

JONATHAN LANGLEY
NURSERY RHYMES
~Book One~

Mog the forgetful cat
Written and illustrated by
Judith Kerr

I Want My Potty
Tony Ross

One Little Teddy Bear
Mark Burgess

ONE SNOWY NIGHT
NICK BUTTERWORTH

AFTER THE STORM
NICK BUTTERWORTH
WITH FOLD-OUT POSTER

Paddington's
1 2 3
MICHAEL BOND
Illustrated by John Lobban

Peter Curry
The big red bus ride

for you to enjoy.